D0528405

For my dearest Rikka

First published 1992 by
Walker Books Ltd
87 Vauxhall Walk
London SE11 5HJ

This edition published 2001

4 6 8 10 9 7 5 3

© 1992 Jez Alborough

Printed in Singapore

All rights reserved

British Library Cataloguing in Publication Data:
a catalogue record for this book
is available from the British Library

ISBN 0-7445-8165-6

WHERE'S MY TEDDY?

Jez Alborough

WALKER BOOKS
AND SUBSIDIARIES
LONDON · BOSTON · SYDNEY

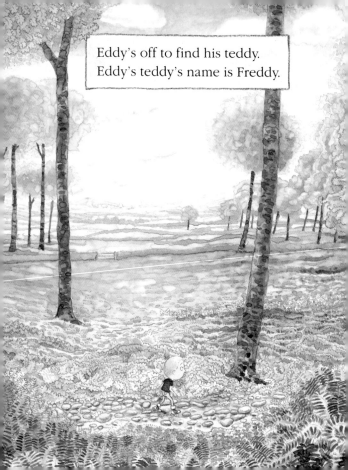

Eddy's off to find his teddy.
Eddy's teddy's name is Freddy.

He lost him in the wood somewhere.
It's dark and horrible in there.

"Help!" said Eddy. "I'm scared already!
I want my bed! I want my teddy!"

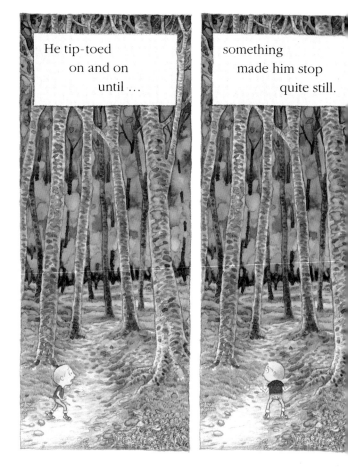

He tip-toed
on and on
until …

something
made him stop
quite still.

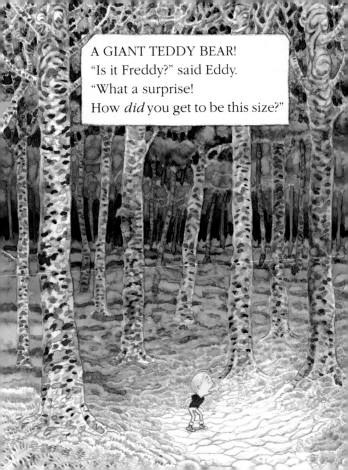

A GIANT TEDDY BEAR!
"Is it Freddy?" said Eddy.
"What a surprise!
How *did* you get to be this size?"

"You're too big to huddle and cuddle," he said,

"and I'll never fit both of us into my bed."

Then out of the darkness,
clearer and clearer,
the sound of a sobbing
came nearer and nearer.

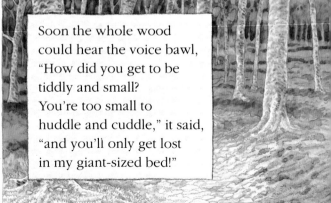

Soon the whole wood
could hear the voice bawl,
"How did you get to be
tiddly and small?
You're too small to
huddle and cuddle," it said,
"and you'll only get lost
in my giant-sized bed!"

It was a gigantic bear and a tiddly teddy stomping towards …

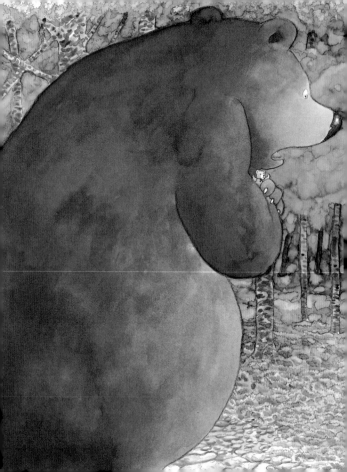

the giant teddy and Eddy.

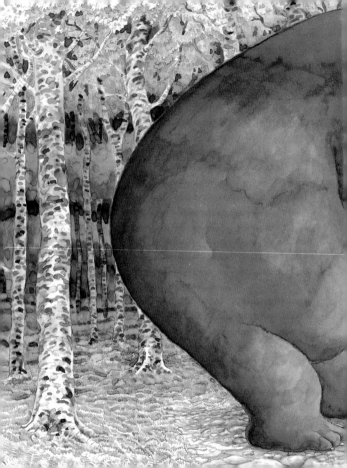

"A BOY!"
yelled the bear.
"MY TEDDY!"
cried Eddy.

all the way back
to their snuggly beds,
where they huddled
and cuddled their
own little teds.